KNOW-ALL NANCY
by TONY GARTH

Nancy was the sort of little girl who knew absolutely everything.

At least she thought she did.

One day, Nancy went on a guided tour of the museum.

The museum was full of old and interesting things. The guide explained what everything was and answered any questions.

"This, ladies and gentlemen, is a suit of armour worn by brave knights of old when they went into battle."

"Er, excuse me," said Nancy, in a know-all way. "I think you'll find that it's actually an ancient bee hive. The bees fly into the top and the honey comes out of a hole near the bottom."

The guide gave Nancy an odd sort of look and moved quickly on to the next exhibit.

"On your left," said the guide, "is a mummy from Ancient Egypt. Our experts say it is over 4,000 years old!"

"In that case, they must have got it wrong," interrupted Nancy. "It is, in fact, a life-sized doll used to teach first aid to nurses in South America."

The guide gave Nancy a very hard stare.

"The next exhibit," continued the guide, "is an old steam engine, dating from the 19th century."

"No, no, no!" said Nancy. "That's not a steam engine. It's a musical instrument. You blow into one end and it makes a noise like a giant trumpet."

"What an irritating little girl," the guide muttered to himself. He was getting very angry now.

In the next room, Nancy spotted a waste paper bin standing by the wall.

"Aha! Now, ladies and gentlemen," she said, in a loud voice. "This exhibit is very interesting. I bet you can't guess what it is."

No one answered. It was perfectly obvious what it was.

"It's an old fashioned time-machine," Nancy announced. She climbed inside. "I'll show you how it works," she said, as she closed the lid behind her.

But by now the group had moved on into the next room, leaving Nancy behind.

So they didn't see a man come along, pick up the bin and move it back to where it belonged...in the dinosaur exhibition!

Slowly, Nancy opened the lid and peeped out. She couldn't believe her eyes. She gulped loudly.

"It really is a time-machine," she whispered. "And it's taken me back to prehistoric times."

She climbed out of the bin and peered around. There was no-one there, apart from herself...

...and lots of very large dinosaurs.

The dinosaurs were made of plastic but Nancy didn't know that. They looked very real to her. She began to feel rather scared.

Suddenly, one of the dinosaurs opened its mouth and gave a VERY LOUD roar. Nancy shrieked and ran back to the time-machine.

"I want to go home," she wailed.

Just as Nancy was climbing back into the time-machine, she heard a voice coming towards her. It sounded familiar.

"And this, ladies and gentlemen, is our pride and joy," the voice said. "Our brand-new dinosaur exhibition." It was the tour guide.

"Help! Help!" shouted Nancy, as she ran towards him. "Save me! Save me! The dinosaurs are after me!"

Then she stopped. "But how did you get here?" she asked, in a trembling voice. "Did you find another time-machine?"

"You silly girl," the tour guide said. "There was no time-machine. And these aren't real dinosaurs. They're made of plastic." Everyone laughed.

"I knew that," Nancy said.

Collect all 30 titles in the Little Monsters series